My best friends

For: Susan and Ralph
From: A.T.B.

First published in Great Britain in 2003
by Zero To Ten, part of Evans Publishing Group
2A Portman Mansions
Chiltern Street
London W1U 6NR
Copyright ©2003 Zero To Ten Ltd
Text copyright ©2003 Anna Nilsen
Illustrations copyright ©2003 Emma Dodd

First published in paperback in 2005

British library cataloguing in Publication Data

Nilsen, Anna, 1948-
  My Best Friend - (My favourite people)
  1. Friendship - Pictorial works - Juvenile fiction
  2. Children's stories - Pictorial works
  I. Title
  823.9'14[J]
  ISBN 1 84089 372 9

Printed in China by WKT Co. Ltd.

My best friends

Written by Anna Nilsen
Illustrated by Emma Dodd

Best friends smile and say hello,

and hold each other's hand.

Best friends laugh and dance at parties...

This is fun!

...and play games like hide and seek.

Best friends give each other presents...

... and share their favourite toys.

Best friends put on grown-ups' shoes when they play at dressing up.

... and swoosh and splash in paddling pools.

Best friends take each other home for tea, and always share their treats and sweets.

Best friends sometimes fall out and fight...

... but soon make up and have a hug.

Best friends get tired
and angry...

Best friends tell each other secrets.

**Some best friends stay
friends for ever.**